RETURN TO SENDER

Return to Sender

written and illustrated by

Kevin Henkes

Greenwillow Books, New York

Library of Congress Cataloging in Publication Data

Henkes, Kevin.
Return to sender.
Summary: When Whitaker writes a letter to
Frogman, a TV super hero, his family laughs,
but they stop laughing and start wondering
when he receives an answer.
[1. Heroes—Fiction] I. Title.
PZ7.H389Re 1984   [Fic]   83-16567
ISBN 0-688-02571-4
ISBN 0-688-02573-0 (lib. bdg.)

For Susan,

————————————————

and in memory of
the Milwaukee Braves

CONTENTS

1 • Dear Frogman   1

2 • Who Believes   8

3 • An Unpleasant Morning   15

4 • New Clothes   24

5 • Pimple and Squash   31

6 • More Proof   41

7 • A Father and Son Talk   48

8 • Rise and Shine   56

9 • Room 103   63

10 • An After-Dinner Discovery   70

11 • The Big F   79

12 • Floor Poison   90

13 • Passing Time   97

14 • A Change of Plans   104

15 • The Day Before Tomorrow   110

16 • On and On   116

CHAPTER 1

Dear Frogman

IT ALL STARTED when Whitaker Murphy sent a letter to Frogman. "Honey," said his mother, "I really think it's just a waste of time." His father said, "Listen, Whit, it can't hurt to try. Just don't feel bad if you don't get an answer." Molly, his little sister, screamed and said that she'd die if Frogman wrote back. That was all the incentive he needed.

Whitaker wasn't sure where Frogman lived, so he simply wrote the words

$$FROGMAN—SUPER\ HERO$$

in large capital letters across an envelope, put his own return address in the upper left-hand corner, stuck on plenty of stamps, and mailed it at the box downtown.

When Orson Pitt, the head clerk at the post office, saw the envelope, he grumbled and groaned. "It's things like this that slow up the service," he muttered as he stamped *Return to Sender, Not Deliverable As Addressed* on the envelope. "Dumb kids."

Then the letter was placed in one of the cubbyholes in the shelves above Barney Edwards's desk. He was Whitaker's mailman.

Barney first noticed the letter as he shuffled up the Murphy front walk. He saw the stamp. And he saw the words FROGMAN—SUPER HERO. He chuckled. Barney knew the Murphy children and he was certain that Whitaker would be terribly disappointed if he didn't get a reply, so he gingerly put the letter in his shirt pocket and continued on his route.

That night at home, after a dinner of three grilled cheese sandwiches, apple slices, corn chips, and cinnamon ice cream, Barney opened the envelope and read the letter. It said:

Dear Frogman,

Were you born a frog? Do you really live underwater? Is your skin *really* green? Or is it fake?

Your friend,
Whitaker Murphy

P.S. My sister Molly is afraid of you.

P.S.S. She thinks you are slimy and ugly.

Barney found some stationery, took out his old Remington typewriter, and wrote this reply:

Dear Mr. Murphy,

Yes, I was born a frog. Yes, I really live underwater, but just part of the time. And yes, my skin is *really* green.

Your amphibious* friend,

Frogman

P.S. *I* am not afraid of *Molly*.

P.S.S. I am not slimy and ugly.

*Go ahead and look that up in your dictionary!

Just for fun, Barney signed Frogman's name in green magic marker. After addressing the envelope to Whitaker, Barney sprinkled a few drops of water on it, blurring the letters a bit, for a touch of authenticity. Then he set the envelope on the kitchen table, next to his vitamins, so that he wouldn't forget it in the morning.

The late-August sun was hidden behind Franklinville, Wisconsin's tallest structure—the water tower—by the time Barney turned the corner onto Kewaunee Street. Whitaker lived on Kewaunee—third from the corner— in the square blue house with the long, rambling porch. Ivy leaves, like musical notes, sang their way up and down and around the railings.

Whitaker and Molly were sitting on the porch steps, waiting for Barney.

"See, Molly," Whitaker explained, pointing to the water tower, "it really is a spaceship. It's just disguised as a water tower."

"I don't believe you," Molly said as she dressed her doll and carefully brushed its golden hair.

Whitaker raised his hands in disgust. "Why else do you think it's painted silver or has that red light that blinks on and off at night, then?"

Molly looked at Whitaker. "Last time you scared me, Daddy told me that the light is so airplanes don't hit it in the dark."

"WRONG," Whitaker protested. He took the doll away from Molly and held it by its hair. "This dumb doll is really one of the space creatures. And tonight while you're asleep, it's going to turn green like Frogman and eat you!"

Molly didn't even try to get her doll back. She just ran into the house, shrieking, "MO-O-O-O-o-o-o-om!"

Whitaker was too absorbed in tying knots in the doll's hair to see Barney, who was already approaching the porch. "Boy, oh boy," Barney said, "it looks like Molly saw a ghost, or a spider, or Frogman, or . . ."

Whitaker turned around quickly and got to his feet, dropping the doll. "Frogman? You know him, Barney?"

"Well, not personally. But it seems to me I've heard of him." He paused. "I'll bet you want the mail."

"Only if it's for me," Whitaker answered anxiously.

"Let me see," Barney said. "There's a postcard from your Aunt Nancy and Uncle Iggie. They're traveling in New York. The picture's of that famous Miss Liberty statue."

"What else?" Whitaker asked.

"Well, I see what appears to be a phone bill. *And* . . ."

"What?"

"One for you."

Barney held out the envelope to Whitaker. Whitaker snatched it excitedly. He tore open the envelope and saw the signature of his hero, written in what he thought was a perfectly disgusting shade of green. "Wow!" he shouted. He dashed inside the house, letting the screen door slam. "MO-O-O-O-o-o-o-om!"

Barney smiled. He finished reading the postcard, and put it and the phone bill in the mailbox. Then he whistled his way down Kewaunee, the water tower looming in the distance.

CHAPTER 2

Who Believes

"SEE? I KNEW HE'D answer me!" Whitaker
said, as he held up the letter so Mrs. Murphy
could read it while she scrubbed the remains
of burned scrambled eggs from a frying pan.

"Well, there has to be a catch," Mrs. Murphy reasoned. She plopped the pan back into

the dishwater, wiped her hands, and took the letter from Whitaker.

"Be careful with it," Whitaker said, wondering if his mother's hands were perfectly dry. Hoping that they were.

"The postmark is smudged—so that's no help," she said. She reread the letter aloud and examined the signature. "Oh, Whit, I don't know about you. Are you sure you just didn't get someone to do this for you?"

"Yes. I'm *sure*. Barney brought it. You can even ask him."

"Well, I don't know. We'll have to let your father take a look at it when he comes home from work. I have a feeling it's just another one of your tricks." She paused, then added, "At least I *think* it is."

Whitaker sighed. He took the letter from his mother and carefully held it in his open hands as he walked down the hallway to Molly's room. He thought that he *might* have heard his mother shout from the kitchen,

"And Whitaker, please don't scare your sister with that thing." But he pretended that he hadn't.

After making Molly cry three times, Whitaker went to his room and closed the door. Lying on his bed, he studied the letter. Then he reached for the dictionary his parents had given him on his last birthday. It sat on the bookshelf beside his bed—dusty from neglect. Following the A's until he came to the word "amphibious," Whitaker read the definition: "able to live both on land and in water." Wow, Whitaker thought.

He traced the signature with his finger, imagining himself right alongside Frogman, fearlessly hopping to the rescue of the oppressed—knocking out Black Beetle and Sergeant Snakehead and The Army Ants with that rapid-fire tongue. Then, together, they'd triumphantly croak a victory song, silhouetted against the orange glow of sunset. The pictures in his head danced him to a late-morning nap. He dreamed of wars and insects, and of course frogs.

That night when Whitaker showed the letter to his father, Mr. Murphy's brow wrinkled in puzzlement.

"I'll be darned," he said, shaking his head. "It looks like that hero of yours really *is* super." He held the letter up to the floor lamp that stood next to the sofa where they sat, taking full advantage of the light.

"I don't think Mom believes it's real," Whitaker whispered.

"It's real all right. But I wonder where it came from."

"Dad," Whitaker impatiently explained, as if the whole world should have known, "it came from Frogman, who is on TV every Saturday morning, who I think I saw last week in the creek by the spaceship at Horlick's Field, who—"

"Wait a minute, Whitaker James," Mr.

Murphy interrupted. "I don't question the fact that Frogman is on TV every Saturday morning. And I admit, I didn't discourage you from writing to him—although maybe I should have. But you never saw a six-foot frog with a cape in the creek at Horlick's Field. *And* that spaceship is a water tower. Nothing else."

Molly, who had been hiding behind the sofa listening, suddenly popped up. "I told you, Whitaker. I told you," she said. She jumped onto the sofa and crawled into Mr. Murphy's lap. "Tell him again, Daddy."

"Tell *her* that this letter is real," Whitaker said. "Dad, you said it was real." He turned toward Molly and added, "And if little sisters touch it, they get warts." He brushed the envelope against Molly's cheek, picturing her face covered with a thousand enormous green pimples.

"Tell him it's not real," Molly pleaded.

"Tell her it *is,*" Whitaker demanded.

"Well . . ." began Mr. Murphy, very slowly, thinking very fast.

"Well?" Whitaker said.

"Well?" Molly said.

"Well . . ." Mr. Murphy repeated. "Let's go ask your mother."

Whether anyone else believed in it or not, the letter from Frogman immediately became Whitaker's most prized possession. It was more valuable to him than his Brewer batting helmet or his baseball autographed by Hank Aaron. More valuable than his dead bug collection or his fiberglass knife with its real cowhide sheath. And even more valuable than his jar of black sand that Aunt Nancy and Uncle Iggie brought back from their trip to Hawaii.

Whitaker put the letter under his pillow at night. During the day, he folded it in half and in half once more, and kept it in his front pocket along with his usual assortment of front pocket necessities—a cat's-eye marble, an inch-thick rubber band, a few baseball cards, a picture of Frogman cut from the back of a box of Colonel Cornflakes, a flattened penny, and a dead wasp or fly to add to his collection.

Whitaker read and reread the letter nearly a hundred times, so that in a matter of days the creases started to give way. Soon the letter was in four wrinkled and ripped and tattered pieces. Whitaker knew what that meant. It was time to write to Frogman again.

CHAPTER 3

An Unpleasant Morning

WHITAKER'S SECOND LETTER to Frogman was written and mailed—in the same fashion as the first—before his parents had a chance to talk with him about what kinds of things in life are real, what kinds are make-believe, and how to tell the difference.

This time, Whitaker asked Frogman how many flies he ate daily. How old he was. And if *he* had a little sister, and weren't they a pain?

As he walked back from the mailbox downtown, Whitaker decided to take better care of the new reply when he received it. He wouldn't fold it or stash it under his pillow. I know, he thought, I'll keep it in the exact middle of my dictionary. Whitaker was pleased. In his entire life he had never had any desire to use a dictionary, and now within a few days he had actually looked up a word, and believe it or not, he had discovered an even better use for it—a safe home for his anticipated letter.

As the previous time, Orson Pitt was the first person to take notice of the new letter. Again, he stamped the envelope *Return to Sender, Not Deliverable As Addressed*. But this time he gave it to Barney personally.

"Edwards," Orson screeched, pushing his

glasses up his thin carrot of a nose, "I'd appreciate it if you'd tell this Whitaker Murphy person to stop this nonsense. I can tell by his unskilled penmanship that he isn't more than a bothersome child, plagued by juvenile stupidity."

Barney laughed out loud—a hearty, rolling laugh. "He's just a little kid with an active and trusting imagination."

Orson turned to Barney and placed the envelope in his outstretched hand. "And kids like that grow up to be people like you—silly adults who forget their age."

Barney gave Orson the best kind of smile he knew how.

"Don't smile at me, Edwards," Orson mumbled. "I hate it."

"Is that so?" Barney singsonged, as he strolled to his desk, the letter already safe in his pocket.

Two days later, Mrs. Murphy emptied Whitaker's pants pockets for the weekly laundry. As always, she was amazed at how much he was able to cram into them. And as always, she was disgusted at how dirty and smelly most of it was. This time, the best, in Whitaker's eyes—and worst, in his mother's—was a half-smoked cigar. He had found it on Monday near the train tracks that ran diagonally through Horlick's Field, and was saving it for the perfect time for a first cigar. That's one of those special things that you simply don't rush. The moment must be exactly right.

"Whitaker? What in heaven's name are you doing with this filthy thing?" Mrs. Murphy asked. She was holding the cigar with two fingers, her pinky sticking straight out. Her nose was scrunched up.

"Oh, that's a cigar," Whitaker answered innocently. He sat at the kitchen table behind a big bowl of soggy cornflakes. Until his mother appeared from the laundry room, he had been flicking the wilted flakes with his spoon against the refrigerator.

"I know what it is. The question is, what are you doing with it?"

"Um, I found it."

"Terrific. Go on."

Thinking quickly, Whitaker said, "I thought Grandpa might like it. I thought I'd save it for his next birthday. For a present."

"I think Grandpa will survive without this particular surprise." Mrs. Murphy rolled her eyes as she walked to the sink. "It is a blessing that school starts next week," she said to herself, in a voice loud enough for her son to hear.

Whitaker wasn't terribly disappointed at the sound of a potential milestone in his life being noisily devoured by the garbage disposal. He was certain that he could find another. And anyway, there were more important things to be concerned with—like the morning's mail. And Lincoln Elementary. Shoot.

Nevertheless, the breakfast encounter left Whitaker moping on the front porch. He looked up at the sky, staring. Instead of frogs or spaceships or County Stadium, the cumulus islands looked like books and desks and fat Miss Smathers, who would be his teacher this year. Even Barney took on a new appearance as he sauntered up the walk. For an instant, he reminded Whitaker of Mr. Wolfe, the principal of Lincoln Elementary, known for his short temper and sly mind. Why, he even had the nerve to slink through the halls during bubbler break and hide in the janitor's room. Then the minute Whitaker or one of his friends—Jeff Hunter or Gordy Lucas—had a perfect spray of water directed at one of the girls, Mr. Wolfe would jump out and drag the offender to the office. He had caught Whitaker seventeen times last year.

"What's the matter, Whitaker?" Barney asked. "If you'd stand on your head, you'd be wearing the biggest smile I've ever seen."

"School starts next week. And I hate it. And I don't want to go. And I'm not going to."

Barney set down his mail sack, took off his hat, and ran his fingers through his thinning gray hair. "Life's chock-full of things that seem unpleasant. Like school. And sirens that wake you in the black-middle of night. And discarded nails, carelessly lying on the sidewalk, that puncture your bike tires and make them go flat. What you have to remember is that things that seem unpleasant usually aren't all bad. Nails come in darn handy for hanging pictures on a wall. Sirens are necessary to get speedy help to someone in need. And school, well school is one place where you learn about life. How big the dinosaurs really were. What state was the thirtieth to become part of this country. The life cycle of the frog. So you see, it's not all boring. And *some* things—the best kinds—you don't even learn from books. In fact, I learned the most during recess. And that's definitely part of school."

Whitaker wasn't totally convinced, but Barney's words comforted him enough at least to let his mind drift back to matters of present importance. "Any mail for me, Barney?"

"I hate to disappoint you, Whitaker," Barney replied. Taking a deep breath and shrugging his shoulders, he continued, "But all there is today is this mailing from the new shopping mall for their first annual back-to-school sale. Were you expecting anything in particular?"

"I was waiting for a letter from a friend. An answer to one I wrote."

"Well, sometimes it takes a while for someone to answer a letter. For example, I had been planning to write a letter last night, myself, but it was inadvertently postponed. You see, after dinner I took out my lawn chair to watch the sunset from my backyard. I only meant to stay out a few minutes. But the colors were magnificent. Red and orange and purple scudding around and around. And before I knew it, the sun was gone and right before my eyes were the most stars I'd ever seen. Dusted over the dark blue, they were slivers of glass, just winking away. I fell asleep and didn't wake until the sun was back where the Eastern stars had been. Sometimes I think I could watch it all forever. So anyway, I didn't write my letter. And maybe the very same thing happened to your friend."

"I doubt it. I don't think my friend would be doing that."

"Well, you never know. But about that letter—the best thing you can do is check again tomorrow. And I have a feeling that it will be here." Barney replaced his hat on his head, his sack already reslung over his shoulder.

Whitaker followed Barney down the steps. Then he lay on the front lawn. He watched the clouds glide past the water tower. He thought about spaceships. He thought about the letter. He thought about school. He found the cloud that resembled Miss Smathers again. Then he pointed his finger and held his hand as if it was a gun. And he shot her.

CHAPTER 4

New Clothes

IT HAD BEEN A BAD DAY all around for Whitaker. First his cigar had been confiscated. Next he had been reminded that school was soon to begin. He hadn't gotten any mail. Then his mother made ham for dinner and managed to ruin it by smothering it with pineapple chunks and brown sugar.

And to top it all off, right when he was in the middle of an after-dinner baseball game at Horlick's Field with his friends (possibly the last of the summer), he heard the telltale rumbling of the family car getting closer and closer. His parents and Molly drove up in their beat-up '64 Chevy Impala. Everyone in the neighborhood called it the Zebra, because it was white with striped primer marks stretching across the body from fender to fender.

"Hey, Champ," Mr. Murphy called from the car, "we're going to the new shopping mall to get school clothes. And that means you, too."

"But, Dad, I can't," Whitaker yelled from second base. "We're in the middle of a game. Tie score."

"I think this is more important. So let's go. Now!"

"Da-a-ad," Whitaker whined, his eyes pleading.

Mr. Murphy did his noted two-finger whistle. And not another word had to be spoken.

Whitaker took off toward the car, his friends waving good-bye behind him.

Within a minute, the Zebra—fully occupied—was cruising in the direction of the mall, the lack of a muffler announcing their presence all the way there.

The parking lot glowed with the festive signs of a grand opening. There was a marching band weaving through the cars, playing "Roll Out the Barrel." Streams of colorful flags and banners, strung from the light poles, flowed above the cars. Attendants in striped uniforms were tying balloons to the car antennas. And there were clowns passing out candy at the entrances.

When the wind blew, light as it was, the banners, flags, and balloons fluttered. "Look!" Molly said. "They're different flavors of birds that are ready to fly away."

"That's stupid," Whitaker said.

Mrs. Murphy clicked her tongue and turned her head to give Whitaker a five-second stare.

"They look like birds to me," she said. "Very pretty ones at that."

"Oh, yeah, birds—pretty ones," Mr. Murphy said, after his wife nudged his arm.

Oh, great, Whitaker thought. First they force me away from the baseball game and now they gang up on me. He wondered, too, how his parents could say that the flags were birds, but not believe that Frogman wrote him that letter.

After circling the lot five times, Mr. Murphy spotted a parking space. It seemed to be ten blocks away from the stores.

Mrs. Murphy made sure that the car doors were locked before saying, "You know how I hate big parking lots—so many cars and careless drivers—and we do have a long walk, so, Whitaker, please hold Molly's hand."

Whitaker took Molly's hand in his own and began to squeeze it so tightly that Molly decided she was old enough to walk through the lot unguarded.

A clown, who said his name was Rosco,

greeted the Murphys as they entered the mall.

"Hello, cute little girl!" he said to Molly, handing her a lollipop. Molly wanted the lollipop badly, but she was too frightened to grab it. It's one thing to see a clown on television, or at the circus sitting twenty rows from the action. But to be face to face with that white skin and those big, decorated eyes and a nose like a bloodied Ping-Pong ball, well, it's not so amusing.

Molly ran to Mrs. Murphy and hugged her legs, whimpering.

Rosco, rather hurt, gave the lollipop to Whitaker, along with one for him. Both of the lollipops were red.

"I don't want this one," Whitaker said. "I want a green one, please."

Rosco, disbelieving at how difficult children could be, shook his painted head and traded a green lollipop for one of the red ones.

Whitaker forgot to say thank you, but he

did remember to step on Rosco's gigantic feet as he passed the clown. Whitaker didn't mind making Molly cry—in fact he rather enjoyed it—but when some stranger did it, it upset him.

Once inside, Mr. Murphy decided that they had better start at the big department store. That way they could get most of their shopping done at one place and avoid unnecessary walking.

Whitaker was first.

"These pants look fine. What do you think?" Mrs. Murphy held up a pair of blue and red plaid corduroys, and waited for an answer from her husband.

"I think they stink," Whitaker said. "I like my own pants."

"I think they're pretty," Molly said.

"They might—fine as they are—be a bit too flashy for Whit, here," Mr. Murphy said.

"Well, I would like him to look decent at school," Mrs. Murphy explained. She rummaged through the shelves and racks. "Now this is nice." It was a matching set. Brown and white checked pants. And a tan shirt with a brown hippopotamus sewn on the pocket.

"That's cute," Molly said.

"That's sick," Whitaker said. "It's for babies."

Mr. Murphy tried to hide a smile as he spoke. "Couldn't we find something a little less . . . *nice?*"

After wearing out four clerks, Whitaker was the not-so-proud owner of two new pairs of green jeans (in honor of Frogman), eight pairs each of T-shirts and socks, and a gray hooded sweatshirt.

Molly wasn't nearly as much trouble. She and her mother had quite similar tastes in clothing. So she ended up with the frilliest and laciest items Mrs. Murphy could find. It was certain: Molly would be a shoo-in for the title of best-dressed kid at The-Cow-Jumped-over-the-Moon Nursery School.

CHAPTER 5

Pimple
and Squash

"LET'S GO OUT A DIFFERENT WAY—not the same way we came in," Mrs. Murphy said, wanting to avoid meeting Rosco again.

As sometimes happens between parents, Mr. Murphy knew exactly what Mrs. Murphy was thinking and agreed immediately.

So the four of them rambled through the mall, surrounded by trees in large ceramic pots and elaborate water fountains. Massive basins of tile caught the sprayed water on its downward tumble. Artificial flowers and real goldfish made their homes in the swirling water.

Whitaker knelt down beside one of the water basins and snatched a goldfish. Just as he was about to place it gently in his bulging pocket, Mr. Murphy grabbed his hand and pried it open above the pool. The fish fell back into the water.

"Why did you do that?" Whitaker asked.

"Because it didn't belong to you," Mr. Murphy answered.

"Could we find out who it belongs to, then, so I can ask them if I can have it?"

Mr. Murphy simply sighed and said something about "kids," in a muffled voice. Whitaker knew that that meant no.

They passed a cookie shop, a candy store, a video arcade, and a pet shop. Each was well worth stopping at as far as Molly and Whitaker were concerned. They begged and cajoled. Wheedled and coaxed.

"Just one cookie?" Molly asked.

"If you let me play *Astro Confusion*, I won't shoot my cornflakes around the kitchen anymore," Whitaker bargained.

"My lollipop's got fuzz on it from when I dropped it. Can I get a new one?"

"Dad, we really could use a watchdog. Don't you think?"

"Mommy, lookit the kitties!"

"Maybe they have frogs! Can I get one?" Whitaker remembered to add, "Please?"

"Pretty please with sugar on top?" Molly said, trying to surpass her brother.

". . . and spaghetti sauce and hot fudge and frogs and . . ."

Figuring that giving in a *little* would be better in the long run, Mr. and Mrs. Murphy sped Whitaker and Molly through the shops faster than water slides down a greased mountain. They did, however, end up with two chocolate chip cookies, a bag of lemon drops, two quarters worth of *Astro Confusion, and*—best of all—two free snails from the pet shop, their grand-opening special (they were out of frogs).

And as if that wasn't enough, when they reached the Zebra, there were two balloons tied to the coat hanger that functioned as a makeshift antenna. One was green and the other was blue.

"I get the green one," Whitaker said.

Molly didn't argue.

At home, Whitaker and Molly—balloons in hand—sat down in the middle of the living room floor. The snails, two small grayish-green lumps, sat between them.

"I'm the oldest, so I get the biggest one," Whitaker said.

Molly didn't argue.

Whitaker named his snail Squash because his shell was dented, as if someone had stepped on him. Molly called hers Pimple because he had a tiny bump on the middle of his shell. And then they had a race.

Whitaker and Molly lined Pimple and Squash on the edge of the braided rug and said, "Go!" But neither snail did much of anything. Squash just poked his head in and out of his shell. And Pimple just rocked from side to side.

"They're not very fast," Molly said, rather disappointed.

"They're snails, they're supposed to be slow," Whitaker replied, with all the sureness of a learned scientist. "But they should at least move forward. A little." He urged them and pushed them and tapped their shells, but nothing more happened.

While they were waiting for a winner, Whitaker took his balloon, tied it in his hair, and tried to watch it float up. He helped Molly do the same, only pulling her hair once or twice.

"I think yours is higher than mine," Molly said.

"That's because I'm taller," Whitaker boasted. "And you know what?" he added proudly, "I always will be. I'm older."

Molly didn't argue.

"What should we do now?" Molly asked. Whitaker shrugged his shoulders. He glanced at the inactive snails, wishing that they were motorized. And that's when he got his idea.

He picked up Squash and tied the string from his balloon around the shell. He held Squash down on the rug and said, "Five . . . four . . . three . . . two . . . one . . . Blast-off!" The balloon slowly rose with Squash attached, poking his head in and out. "They won't race on the ground, but we can race them in the air!" Whitaker exclaimed. "See?"

Molly's eyes and mouth widened with amazement. Whitaker assisted her in preparing Pimple for his takeoff. Then Whitaker climbed up onto the couch to reach Squash, who was now hanging in midair, the balloon having been stopped by the ceiling.

When both snails were ready, Whitaker said, "On your mark, get set, go! First one to the ceiling is the winner."

It was usually a tie. Except when Whitaker held Squash above his head.

"That's cheating," Molly complained.

"I know," Whitaker said.

By the time Whitaker and Molly were ready for bed, Pimple and Squash had survived more races than most snails could handle. The new pets were wished numerous good nights before being placed on the kitchen counter in an empty fish tank, to which was added some soil, leaves, a twig, lettuce, and a tiny dish of water. Close-by, the balloons, secured to the spindles of one of the kitchen chairs, kept watch throughout the night.

Molly was the first one up the next morning. Before she washed her face or combed her hair, she went to say good morning to

Pimple and Squash. Pimple was rocking from side to side as usual, but Squash just lay there, still as a small gray rock.

Molly had pulled a chair up to the counter and was leaning over the snails when Whitaker entered the kitchen. He pushed Molly aside to get a full view of Pimple and Squash. When Squash refused to return Whitaker's greetings, Whitaker picked up the snail and shook him and nudged him and talked to him—without the hoped-for result. Squash didn't poke his head in and out. He didn't move at all. Nothing.

"You killed him," Whitaker said to Molly.

"No," Molly answered quietly.

"You killed him because he was bigger than yours, and didn't have a stupid pimple on his back. I hate you."

"No," Molly insisted. "I found him like that. Maybe he just sleeps late."

In a fit of rage and sadness and jealousy, Whitaker flushed Squash down the toilet, and when Molly wasn't looking, tied Pimple to her balloon, opened the back door, and let them fly away.

"Where's Pimple and where's my balloon?" Molly asked.

"A ghost came and took them away," Whitaker said, pointing out the window.

Holding back tears, Molly ran to the window and spotted Pimple and her balloon sailing upward until the branches of the apple tree in their backyard ended their flight.

"Look," Molly shouted, "the ghost didn't get very far. Will you help me get them back?"

Thinking that by rescuing Pimple, he'd rightfully deserve partial ownership, Whitaker agreed to climb the tree. Sitting on his favorite branch—Pimple safely rocking in his pocket, the balloon's string wound around his wrist—Whitaker took a deep breath and surveyed the neighborhood. It was early yet, and still. Dew drops covered the lawns. They reminded Whitaker of the way the sun had shone on the water dish in the snail's tank.

Little diamonds of light. He peered downward at the tiny jewels until, unfocused, they blurred in his vision.

"Whitaker," Molly yelled, jumping up and down at the base of the tree, "is my snail okay?"

"*Our* snail is fine," he yelled back.

If ever he needed a letter from a super hero, it was today.

CHAPTER 6

More Proof

BARNEY HAD BEEN NOTICING the signs all morning—the signs that summer was ending and autumn was willing and ready to take over. The leaves were beginning to turn colors around the edges. The wind, as Barney would say, was getting sassy—surprising your face with a nip. And the sun, hot as it still was, was bowing out earlier and earlier, allowing more time for the moon to perform.

As he walked the streets of Franklinville, Barney decided that he was going to have himself one good-time kind of day. And it's certain—if Orson could have seen Barney that morning, he would have blown a fuse.

Barney was wearing his new Brewer baseball cap, not his official mail hat. And, he had eaten his breakfast on the route—three chocolate-frosted doughnuts. That meant chocolate fingerprints on half the mail delivered that morning. Barney even collected aluminum cans along his way, putting them in his sack with the letters, phone bills, and magazines. The thought of drips of Coke or Mountain Dew or Miller Lite defacing the mail never entered Barney's mind. But best of all was what happened in the Campbells' frontyard. Candy and Fletcher were running through their sprinkler, laughing and singing. Barney couldn't resist joining in. So he set down his sack, took off his shoes and socks and hat, rolled up his pants, and darted through the sprinkler with Candy and Fletcher.

It was the most enjoyable morning Barney had had in quite some time.

Meanwhile, Whitaker had convinced Molly that Pimple was a cousin of Frogman and that, like his famous relative, he too was capable of causing warts on little sisters. Although she had grown rather fond of Pimple, she didn't want to risk ruining her complexion, so Molly decided that Whitaker was right—Pimple should be his. Alone.

Whitaker spent the morning waiting for Barney. To make the minutes drag less, Whitaker took a stone and drew a small, lopsided baseball diamond on the cement. Placing Pimple on home plate, Whitaker snapped his fingers to indicate a hit, and then he cheered Pimple on to first base.

As always, Pimple rocked from side to side, nothing else.

Barney, who had been watching quietly, said, "That little fellow sure wouldn't be a very successful base stealer, would he?"

Whitaker turned with a start. "Barney! Did I get my letter?"

"Why, the Murphy family, which of course includes you, got a real haul today." Barney held up a thick stack of envelopes. He cleared his throat and in a robust voice began the mail call."Number one, electric bill," he said, handing the envelope over to Whitaker. "Number two, something from the state motor vehicle department. Numbers three, four, and five, various-sized colored envelopes addressed to your mother. All with very lovely handwriting, I should add."

Whitaker took each piece of mail as Barney announced it. But he was too anxious even to remember what Barney had said two words earlier.

"Number six, a bank statement. Number seven—now this looks interesting."

"What?" Whitaker asked.

"Don't get excited," Barney said. "It's an oversized postcard from your Aunt Nancy and Uncle Iggie. They're still in New York."

Bending down, Barney showed the picture to Whitaker. It wasn't a photograph but simply a fat red apple on a white background. Whitaker wasn't impressed.

"What's so big about an apple?" Whitaker asked, seriously.

"You see," Barney answered, "that's what people call New York City—The Big Apple. Although, for the life of me, I don't know why. As far as I know, The Big Apple is the name of a dance. Maybe they just do a lot of dancing there. Let's read it. Maybe we'll find out."

The postcard said:

Dear ones,

    You wouldn't believe all the big bridges here. Absolutely enormous. Thousands of times bigger than the one over Horlick's Creek. Uncle Iggie had the notion to go fishing off one of them, but a kind officer suggested he didn't.

We went to one of those ballet shows. We never saw so many folks jumping around in all our years. Just like the annual frog jumping contest back home, only with skinny people. Uncle Iggie let me buy a pink tutu, and I wear it as I dance around the hotel room, dusting the furniture. He says I'm quite a sight!

Love always,
Nancy and Iggie

"I guess they do dance there," Whitaker said, eyeing the two pieces of mail that remained in Barney's hand.

"Back to business," Barney continued. "Number eight—" he said, holding one of the envelopes up to the sunlight. The envelope was thin, so Barney could read the enclosed note without much trouble. "This is from the library. It is a notice that says a book called *Psychology and Childhood Development*, that your parents requested, is available to be checked out at their convenience."

Whitaker didn't pay any attention to that. He only hoped that the last envelope was the letter from Frogman.

"Number nine," Barney said, "and remember the last is usually the best. Number nine is for you."

Recognizing the familiar green handwriting, Whitaker was immediately aware that Frogman had responded. "All right!" he yelled, dropping the other eight pieces of mail. "Bye, Barney," Whitaker shouted as he ran up the steps and into the house. Proof, he was thinking, now I have more proof.

CHAPTER 7

A Father and Son Talk

"GOOD NIGHT" MOLLY CALLED from bed, upstairs.

"Good night, Molly, for the twentieth and *last* time," Mr. Murphy shouted back. He sat down at the kitchen table across from Mrs. Murphy and said to her, "Whitaker sure is quiet. It's usually he who yells down all night."

Mrs. Murphy set her teacup gently on the table and ran her finger around its rim. "He was tired out. Being the last Saturday before school starts, he wanted to get his money's worth today—and he did. Jeff and Gordy and he played hard." She fidgeted with a spoon, the sugar bowl, the butter dish. "And then all this Frogman business . . ."

"With school on Monday, I'm sure he'll forget about it soon enough," Mr. Murphy said. He dumped three teaspoons of sugar into his coffee mug and watched it dissolve as he stirred. "It's been a long summer. I think he just needed something new to fill these last days. After all, you can only play so much baseball, and do so much gallivanting with your friends."

"I'd still like to know where this came from," Mrs. Murphy said, holding up the new letter from Frogman. "That other letter was one thing—it didn't faze me—but *two!*"

Mr. and Mrs. Murphy had taken the letter from Whitaker after dinner. They told him that they just wanted to read it over a few times. Whitaker wasn't too keen on the idea, but they promised to return it the following day, so what could he do?

The letter said:

Dear Whitaker,

In answer to your questions . . .

1. Depending on my appetite, I average 999 flies per day.

2. Due to my chosen profession—super-hero—I cannot divulge my true age. Let's just say I'm old enough to be smart enough to remember what it's like to be young.

3. No, I haven't any little sisters (older ones either), but I can imagine that they could be hard to deal with at times, however pretty.

Your amphibious friend,
Frogman

Mrs. Murphy folded the letter and re-placed it in its envelope. "You can't tell me he wrote this. We don't even have a type-writer. And he doesn't know words like di-vulge or—"

"Maybe he does," Mr. Murphy inter-rupted. "You know, he's been spending time with his dictionary lately. The last couple of days I've seen him going through it. And I'll bet the Hunters or the Lucases own a type-writer. You know all the crazy things those kids have gotten into before. This is just an-other one. No big deal. I'm sure it's nothing."

"Do you think it's possible for someone from the Frogman television program to have answered the letters?" Mrs. Murphy asked, suddenly.

Mr. Murphy reexamined the letter and the envelope. "No," he said finally, "there's no special letterhead, and the postmark is local. You know, we're probably reading too much into this. It's *nothing*. If we forget about it, he'll forget about it."

Silence. Both Mr. and Mrs. Murphy toyed with the handles of their respective mug and cup.

"I would feel better if one of us had a talk with him," Mrs. Murphy said, vaguely. "And I think this is the kind of thing a father should handle." She paused. "I just don't want it to get out of hand."

Sighing, Mr. Murphy picked up the letter and put it in his shirt pocket. "Okay," he said, "tomorrow. Tomorrow, we'll talk."

Sunday afternoon. Whitaker and Mr. Murphy were in the backyard playing baseball. At the beginning of the summer, Mr. Murphy had measured a strike zone on the side of the garage and marked it with masking tape.

First Mr. Murphy helped Whitaker with his pitching. Then Mr. Murphy pitched to Whitaker, to help his batting along.

"Whitaker, watch your stance. Move your right foot back a bit," Mr. Murphy instructed from the uneven pitcher's mound that Whitaker had formed with dirt from the garden.

"Dad, do you think I could be a pro when I grow up?" Whitaker asked after watching his father's celebrated curve ball whiz past him. A strike.

"Well, you have to practice real hard to be a pro," Mr. Murphy answered. "I used to want that, but it's not as easy as it may seem."

"It'd be fun," Whitaker said, matter-of-factly.

"I guess. But no matter how much you may dream about it, you have to be good. I just wasn't good enough."

Another strike rocketed past Whitaker.

Mr. Murphy breathed deeply. Trying eventually to lead into a talk about Frogman, he said, "I used to picture myself playing for the Braves with Hank Aaron—playing in the World Series. But it came to the point where I had to be realistic. I had to stop pretending. Pretending's okay to a degree, but it can hold you back and keep you from moving on.

Growing up." He was thinking about Frog-man.

"Are you saying I should give up baseball, already?" Whitaker's voice was touched with disappointment.

"Oh. No, not at all," Mr. Murphy said quickly, frustrated at the thought of mislead-ing Whitaker. "I guess I'm just saying it isn't good to believe in something that isn't real. Do you know what I'm talking about now?"

Whitaker didn't, but he nodded anyway.

"Well, good," Mr. Murphy said, greatly re-lieved. He walked toward Whitaker, took the Frogman letter from his pocket and put it in Whitaker's, and ruffled his hair. "I guess it can't hurt for you to keep this thing then, as a souvenir."

Whitaker was confused. Real/pretend. He hadn't understood what his father had been trying to get at. But before he could ask a question to clear things up, Mr. Murphy said excitedly, "Really, though, about baseball, you're pretty good. And you've got a lot of time. So here's my best pitch."

Mr. Murphy went into an exaggerated windup. Hamming it up. The ball—a bullet—had perfect direction. Whitaker swung at it and made solid contact. Now that's real, Whitaker thought as he watched the ball disappear beyond the trees on Kewaunee Street, and so is my letter from Frogman.

CHAPTER 8

Rise and Shine

THE NIGHT BEFORE THE FIRST DAY of a new school year can be a long one. When the lights go out, the noises seem louder. The shadows seem darker. Even your bed can seem hard and uncomfortable. And then if you have other things on your mind, like a perplexing talk with your father, sleep is not so easy to come by.

It took Whitaker a long time to fall asleep. But once he did, he didn't awaken until the dark was replaced by sunlight, and the noises weren't those of the night but rather those of the morning—chirping birds and his mother's joyous humming.

"Whitaker," Mrs. Murphy said, between melodies, "rise and shine."

"Yeah, get up, Whit," Molly called. "School today! School today!"

"Okay, okay," Whitaker managed to say. He rubbed his eyes, counted to three, and thrust the blankets off his bed. They landed in a rumpled heap on the floor.

Molly was prancing around in the hallway in front of the full-length mirror. She was wearing her new red dresss. Buttons, in the shape of flowers, were evenly spaced, running from the bottom of her chin to the tops of her knees.

"See, I'm all ready," she said, with a curtsy.

"So what?" Whitaker mumbled on his way to the bathroom.

Downstairs, the kitchen was filled with the smells of good things to eat. And despite the thought of having to go to school, Whitaker's appetite was entirely unaffected. There was cinnamon toast, scrambled eggs, bacon, orange juice, and milk. Whitaker had all that plus his daily bowl of Colonel Cornflakes. He tried to go through them as fast as possible; he needed only two more box tops before he could send for a free Frogman Utility Pen that could allegedly squirt water, tell time, and write in gold ink that glowed in the dark.

"Whitaker, if you don't stop eating, you'll be late for school," Mrs. Murphy observed, glancing at the clock above the stove.

"Good idea, huh?" Whitaker said, only half joking.

Mrs. Murphy was collecting the dirty

dishes, banging them on the inside of the trash container, and stacking them in the sink. "Scoot along and brush your teeth," she said to Whitaker. "You've always been my slowpoke, haven't you? Molly got up with your father. She's been ready for what seems like days. And I don't have to take her for another hour. But you—you need prodding."

She grabbed Whitaker's bowl of cornflakes before he had finished them. He hadn't had the chance to fling even *one* cornflake. "Oh," Mrs. Murphy added, "I talked to Mrs. Hunter earlier. She said that Jeff would be waiting for you on his porch at eight-fifteen. And from there you can both walk past Gordy's house. Mrs. Lucas will have him ready by twenty-after. Then the three of you can walk together. Just like last year."

Whitaker ran upstairs with the honest intention of brushing his teeth. But first he went to his room and picked up his dictionary. Page 242. That was the exact middle. And that's where he kept the new letter from

Frogman and the remains of the old one. While he was deciding if he should take the letter to school with him, his eyes darted across the page, from word to word. His favorite words on page 242 were Martian, marzipan, and mash.

"Whitaker James," Mrs. Murphy screamed from the stairway, "hurry up!"

In reflex, Whitaker grabbed the letter and Pimple—forgetting about his teeth—and bounded down the stairs.

Mrs. Murphy immediately spotted Pimple and the letter.

"You cannot bring that snail to school." Cringing, she took Pimple from Whitaker and temporarily set him on the TV. "And that letter—I thought your father had a talk with you about that."

"Oh, he did," Whitaker said, taking off for the front door.

Worried and uncertain how to handle the situation, Mrs. Murphy simply held the door open for Whitaker. She tried to kiss him good-bye, but he slipped out from under her.

"Be good," she called. She watched him until he turned the corner onto Blake Avenue. Molly watched too.

Whitaker stopped at Jeff's house as arranged. Then Jeff and Whitaker stopped at Gordy's house. The three of them walked to Lincoln Elementary together. Just like last year.

On the way, they tossed stones at the stop signs. They wrote the words "Help! Let Me Out!" on the dusty trunks of four cars parked on Summit Avenue. They placed a row of apples (from the orchard on Summit) across the middle of the road, and sat on the curb to wait for a car to drive by and crush them. And they talked about Miss Smathers.

"My mom says that Miss Smathers's first name is Gladys," Gordy said. "My mom also said that they went to school together and that she's been fat all her life."

"Gladys," Whitaker said, grinning, thinking that the name fit her perfectly.

"My sister Joyce says that Miss Smathers can get real mean," Jeff said. "I'll bet if she sat on you, she'd kill you."

"I wish she'd sit on Mr. Wolfe," Whitaker said hopefully, remembering his numerous run-ins with the principal.

"Look, you guys!" Jeff shouted.

A school bus was barreling down Summit, heading straight for the apples. In seconds some of the apples were smashed, bits sent off in all directions. Others rolled haphazardly into the gutter.

"That was the best roadblock ever!" Gordy yelled.

"Roadblock!" Whitaker shrieked. "That's what we should call Miss Smathers."

"Great!" Jeff said. "She sure looks like a roadblock."

"Wait till we tell the rest of the class," Gordy said, smirking.

They laughed the rest of the way.

CHAPTER 9

Room 103

ROOM 103 SMELLED THE WAY Whitaker remembered Room 102 smelling last year—of
chalk and paper and tempera paint and books
and newly sharpened pencils. Twenty-seven
small desks were arranged in five rows—
three rows of five and two rows of six. One

large desk was at the front of the room, facing the twenty-seven small desks. As is typical of a first day of school, the room was very clean and neat and precisely organized. Even the floor shone.

Everyone was there. Whitaker, Jeff, and Gordy. Susan and Bud and Stephanie and Henry and Joey and Franny and Bill and Cynthia and Kathleen and Bruce and Roger and Gertrude and Aaron and Libby and P.J. and Pam and Sam and Frederick and Ava and Webster and Dudley and Ada and Ryan.

There was also a new girl Whitaker didn't know, but soon would.

And of course, Miss Smathers.

"Good morning, children, and welcome to Room 103," Miss Smathers said in greeting. She wrote her name on the blackboard (it was actually dull green) in squat, rounded letters. "I'm Miss Smathers and I'm looking forward to a year of learning and fun with you." When she talked, she enunciated each word so extensively that her mouth appeared to be moving in exaggerated slow motion. Her lips rolling. Teeth protruding.

"Your names are labeled on the upper left-hand corner of each desk. Let's quietly search for our names and sit in our designated seats."

Not so quietly, the children shuffled and climbed around and over the desks until everyone had located his or her own place.

Whitaker ended up in the middle row, second from the front. Kathleen sat on one side of him, P.J. on the other. Gordy sat in front of him and the new girl behind. Jeff was halfway across the room.

"Settle down, settle down," Miss Smathers commanded, slow and loud. Sitting down at her desk and fluffing her hair, she continued in a softer voice, "That's much better. Now, why don't we go up and down each row? Say your name and tell us something about yourself. I'll follow along with my seating chart. That way I can connect your names with your faces, and we'll all be better acquainted."

Henry was first.

"I'm Henry," he said quietly. It's hard to be first, so that's all he said.

Franny was next and less bashful.

"My name is Franny C. Burns. Franny is short for Francine. The C is for Constance. I have a brother, Franklin, who spits his food all over the place. He's one-and-a-half years old." Franny imitated her brother to a delighted response from the other students. Miss Smathers exercised her mouth, and everyone knew that meant to be quiet.

Then came Roger.

"Roger is my first name. Mahoney is my last name. And I'm not saying my middle name because it's stupid."

As to be expected, the students started guessing. "Filbert?" "Delmar?" "Ignatius?"

Once again, Miss Smathers exercised her mouth. Once again, quiet.

Pam told about her trip to Madison. Bruce demonstrated how to tie a square knot using the drawstring from his sweatshirt. Libby, who lived on a farm, told about the birth of her foal Morocco. Ryan, who had six brothers and four sisters, said all their names in order from youngest to oldest. He only had to start over three times.

When it was Jeff's turn, he explained the finer points of creating successful apple roadblocks. He almost told Miss Smathers about how he and Whitaker and Gordy thought "Roadblock" would be a good name for her. But he didn't.

Gordy looked straight at Miss Smathers and said, "My name is Gordon Lucas, but everyone calls me Gordy. My mother's name is Donna Lucas. Before she married my father, William, her name was Donna Hoover. She says she went to school with you and—"

"Next!" Miss Smathers exploded, remembering her school days and not looking forward to Gordy's mother's version of them.

Whitaker, checking to make sure that his prized letter was still in his shirt pocket, was trying to decide if he should tell the class about Frogman's correspondence. He hadn't even told Gordy and Jeff yet. It was one of those things—so special—that you tend to keep to yourself. And anyway, what if no one believed?

Not ready to share his choice information, Whitaker said that he was named after his grandfather, Whitaker James Murphy. He also said that he wished that summer vacation lasted much longer than it did.

"Now!" Miss Smathers exclaimed. "As you probably have realized, behind Whitaker is a new face. New to Lincoln Elementary. New to Franklinville. New to Wisconsin."

Miss Smathers motioned for the girl to rise. The girl did, beaming.

Whitaker turned around to get a better look at her. She was thin, with wispy straw-like blond hair.

"My name is Felicity Cooper," she said, maintaining an enormous smile even as she spoke. "I'm from California and I'm going to be an actress. We moved to Wisconsin because I've never experienced the four seasons the way my father says they were meant to be experienced. I've never seen snow or a cow, except in pictures, and my father thought that this was as good a place as any to see them in person."

"What a very nice story," Miss Smathers said. "And what a very beautiful name you have." Miss Smathers repeated Felicity's name, in song, four times—fluttering her hands in rhythm, eyes closed. "How lucky you are to own that name," she added with envy.

Meaning no harm, Felicity asked, "What is *your* first name, Miss Smathers?"

"Next!" Miss Smathers bellowed, ignoring the question.

Without hesitation, Whitaker screamed, "GLADYS! Her name is GLADYS!"

Instantly, the class was roused and giggling and saying, "Gladys?" "Gladys!" "GLADYS!!"

And guess who had to stay after school, on the very first day?

CHAPTER 10

An After-Dinner Discovery

BECAUSE IT WAS THE FIRST DAY of school, Mrs. Murphy had a tableful of chocolate-chip cookies waiting when Whitaker got home. They were delicious.

And because it was the first day of school and Mrs. Murphy had baked the cookies and was too tired to cook dinner, the Murphys went to the Big Bear Hamburger Heaven to eat. It was delicious, too. At least for a while.

"Should we drive through and eat in the car, or should we eat inside the restaurant?" Mr. Murphy asked.

"In the car," Whitaker said. "That way we get to talk into the bear when we order."

"Yes. Yes. Yes," Molly said in agreement.

Although Mrs. Murphy preferred sitting in the restaurant, she was so delighted that Whitaker and Molly were agreeing that she didn't say a word.

The bear said, "May I take your order?" and "Thank you," and "That will be $9.58," and "Drive around to the side, please."

"How come the bear looks like a boy, but talks like a girl?" Molly asked.

"The bear is a man, but the voice you heard is the lady he ate for dinner," Whitaker said in a serious voice. "And you can be his dessert."

Molly looked horrified. Mrs. Murphy rolled

her eyes. Mr. Murphy snickered and tried to explain to Molly how a lady inside the building was talking into a microphone. And that it only sounded as if she was inside the bear.

Molly was as confused as ever, but by the time she ate her first french fry, the only thing she was thinking about was food.

"Molly told me all about her school, when I came home for lunch," Mr. Murphy said. "But how was your first day, Whit?"

Setting down his Bear Burger with everything, plus extra onions, Whitaker answered, "It was all right. We got a new kid who smiles a lot, who never saw a cow or snow. And we got a lot of old kids, too. And the teacher is fat."

"Your mom says you were a little late coming home after school. Is that right?"

His mouth was full, but Whitaker replied just the same. "I thought I'd help the teacher fix up the room after school. Nice of me, huh?"

"You're sure you weren't in any trouble?"

Whitaker nodded, not wanting to worry his parents.

Molly was playing with her pickle when she asked, "Why do they call them Bear Burgers?"

"Because they're made of dead bears, why do you think?" Whitaker replied, slurping his chocolate shake.

Molly made a horrible face.

"Whit, cut it out," Mr. Murphy said. He tried to reassure Molly. "The owner of the restaurant is named Clayton Bear. And he makes the burgers. So that's why they're called Bear Burgers."

All Molly kept thinking of was her Teddy —between buns with ketchup and mustard—so she gave her burger to Whitaker and concentrated on her fries.

"For some reason, I can't finish my burger, either," Mrs. Murphy said, holding her stomach.

"No problem. I can handle it," Mr. Murphy said.

And he did.

After dinner and ice-cream cones, the noisy Zebra was leisurely driven around the outskirts of town. The sky was splendid. The clouds—thin, dappled strips—lay across a field of dying rose. A chorus of insects made inspired music, but the Zebra's grumbling drowned it out.

"You know," Mrs. Murphy said dreamily, "the night is so lovely, but the sound of this car sort of ruins the effect."

"I'll get at it soon," Mr. Murphy assured her.

"I like it," Whitaker said. "This way people know us all over town, even when we're blocks away."

"Don't I know?" Mrs. Murphy said. She turned around to see why Molly was silent. Molly's head was resting against the back of the seat. Sound asleep. Before turning to the front again, Mrs. Murphy ordered, "Whita-

ker, get your head back inside the window."
He was trying to catch bugs.

As they were nearing home, Whitaker spotted the flashing red light of thc water tower.
He thought about an invasion of space creatures. How some aliens would arrive at
Horlick's Field, and teaming up with Frogman, take Miss Smathers hostage. Then
they'd transport her to some uncharted planet, millions of light years away. Never to be seen
again.

Focusing on that thought, he stared at the water tower, getting closer and closer as they
approached Kewaunee Street.

Even though it was becoming dark, Whitaker could see well enough to notice a difference in the water tower. The massive tank
was as always—spaceship-silver. But the cylindrical legs weren't. They were now
chartreuse. The exact color of Frogman's cape.

"Hey, you guys," Whitaker said, pointing,

"look at the spaceship. It's turning green because Frogman's staying there."

Mr. and Mrs. Murphy turned toward each other, eyes wondering, searching.

"I thought you cleared things up with him," Mrs. Murphy whispered to her husband.

"I thought I did *too*," Mr. Murphy whispered back.

"You guys, look!" Whitaker persisted.

Mr. Murphy parked the car and said sternly, "Listen, Whitaker, there is no such thing as Frogman, except on TV and in comic books. And the water tower—not spaceship—is being painted. I read about it in the newspaper today. And there is no magic about that. At all."

"What about my letters, then?"

"Whitaker, I'm not sure how you or your friends managed that, but you know as well enough as I that they're no more real than if I wrote a letter and said it was from the Easter Bunny."

"Shhh, Dad," Whitaker said with concern. "Molly still believes in him."

"Right, and you used to too. But you grew out of it. Just like you'll grow out of this Frogman business. And please, Whitaker, do it in a hurry. For me. Okay?"

Whitaker didn't answer. It wasn't the same thing as the Easter Bunny, though. It didn't make sense to Whitaker that parents *want* you to believe in things like that, and then they act funny when you believe in something better. He had known for a long time that his parents hid the eggs and candy around the house on Easter Sunday. Not some rabbit. Same for Santa Claus on Christmas. But he also knew that his parents didn't write the Frogman letters. Or why would they be so worried? And Whitaker knew that *he* didn't. So who was left but Frogman?

The last blocks were driven in silence. Mr. and Mrs. Murphy were thinking of how they could convince Whitaker that Frogman wasn't real. Whitaker was thinking of how he

could convince his parents that he was. And
Molly was dreaming that she was Goldilocks,
sitting at a table having dinner with the
Three Bears. It wasn't porridge they were
feasting on. It was burgers.

CHAPTER 11

The Big F

THE REST OF THE WEEK passed as most weeks do—sometimes quickly, sometimes slowly. And it was filled with the things that weeks usually are filled with—some good, some not so good.

But two events transpired of major interest. Number one—Mr. and Mrs. Murphy took possession of Whitaker's letters, in the hope that by doing so, Whitaker would be more apt to forget Frogman and graduate to less fantastic pursuits.

And number two—the water tower's new yellow-green paint job was completed. The entire structure had become a bright vision, to say the least. And to Mr. and Mrs. Murphy's dismay, Whitaker was all the more certain that Frogman had taken up residence in Horlick's Field. According to Whitaker, the "spaceship" was his local headquarters. The color proved it.

And then, what Whitaker saw on Saturday morning was the icing on the cake . . .

A big F.

Whitaker thought that he was seeing things, so he pulled the window shade back down and counted to ten. Saturday morning light filtered into the room, making amber lines on the floor, the wall, the bed, the dresser. Whitaker stared at the lines while he counted, then raised the shade again. It was still there. A large letter F—bold and black—dominated the tank of the water tower.

Dressing in haste, Whitaker continued to glance out the window, to make sure. Then he ran down the stairs two at a time, the wood creaking beneath his weight.

The kitchen was empty, but dirty dishes cluttering the table let Whitaker know that everyone was up. He found his father on the side of the house, trimming the hedge for the last time of the season.

Even though he was sure that the F would convince his skeptical father, Whitaker started slowly. "Morning, Dad," he said cheerfully. "Where's Mom and Molly?"

"Morning, son," Mr. Murphy said, setting down the shears and wiping his forehead. "They went to the grocery store. They're getting hot dogs, potato chips, and marshmallows. We thought that this might be one of the last chances to eat outside. Sort of an end of the summer picnic. What do you think of that?"

"Great," Whitaker replied. He loved grilling-out. Especially when they had marshmallows, toasted dark brown, between two pieces of chocolate and two graham cracker halves.

"Have you gone out in front yet?" Whitaker asked.

"Nope. Why?"

"Will you follow me, Dad? I want to show you something."

Whitaker led his father around the house to the front yard. Raising his head and nodding to the water tower, he exclaimed, "What do you think of that?"

Putting his hands in his pockets, Mr. Murphy said, in a patient voice, "I think the new paint job is nice. But I thought we weren't talking about that anymore."

"But Dad, I mean the F. It stands for Frogman. It's just like the one on his cape. Now you have to believe."

Mr. Murphy's patience was at an end.

"That's enough, Whitaker," he said. "The F is for Franklinville. And I'm sure you know it." Mr. Murphy briskly walked back to the bushes and started to chop ferociously. "And if you want me to play that game, I will," he called. "I think the F stands for frustrated— and that's what I am this very minute."

Mrs. Murphy didn't appreciate Whitaker's observation any more than Mr. Murphy had. Whitaker didn't bother trying to persuade Molly—she was too easy a target. But Barney was another story altogether.

"Not one piece of mail for the Murphy family today," Barney shouted, halfway down the block.

"It doesn't matter," Whitaker said, when Barney was in talking range.

"Everything matters," Barney said, pointing to the large oak in the front yard, "from every leaf on that tree to that monster of a tower over yonder."

Willing to give it one more try, Whitaker asked, "Do you see that large F?" He pointed to the tower.

"Why sure I do. But I'd be willing to place a wager that most folks don't. Some probably never even bothered to notice that this town has a water tower." Barney paused. "And today I'd say that that F is to let us know what a *f*ine day it is. But the look on your face says—*f*orlorn."

Whitaker didn't know what that meant, but it sounded bad.

"What's the matter?" Barney asked.

"It's a long story," Whitaker began. He went on to tell Barney about the two letters he had received from his hero Frogman, and how his parents didn't believe. Whitaker also told about how he thought that Frogman had come to Horlick's Field and how the F proved it. And Whitaker ended by saying that his parents were mad at him, and that he was mad at them, and that he was planning to run

away. To live at Horlick's Field. With Frogman.

For the first time, Barney was aware that
one of his simple plans to bring a little happi-
ness into someone's life wasn't so simple any
longer.

"Now, Whitaker," Barney said, scratching
his head as if to shuffle through all his collected memories in search of the one he
needed, "speaking from experience, I'd ad-
vise against running away. I tried that over a
half-century ago, and I came back real soon."

"I have to Barney," Whitaker said, eyes on
the big F.

"I'm going to tell you something my pa
told me when I was fixing to run off. And
I've never forgotten it. Even told my own
kids when the time came. Pa said to me, 'A
yard without a tree ain't fit for a dog.'"

"But I don't have a dog, Barney." Whitaker sounded puzzled.

Barney laughed. "Let me explain," he

said. "This is where you belong. Here you've got a mom and a dad and a sister and a charming house. Not to mention this mighty oak—the Cadillac of trees. Just like an old hard-luck dog without a tree in his yard—no place out there is going to feel like home. Horlick's Field with Frogman may seem like the place to be, but you'd miss your folks and Molly and your house and even this tree before you could say Frogman ten times."

"But what about the F? Do you believe it stands for Frogman?"

Barney had to be careful how he answered. "I imagine that that F can mean whatever anyone wants it to mean. And the word Frogman seems as good a choice as any."

Whitaker was looking down at his shoes. He'd never realized how filthy they were before. He spit on his fingers and rubbed them over the Nike swooshes on his shoes, trying to get off some of the dirt.

"This Frogman fellow, is he kind of like a hero to you?" Barney asked.

"I guess," Whitaker replied, nodding.

"Well," Barney said, "to tell the truth, heroes can become a disappointing business, because we're really all the same. And that means that we all make mistakes. Even heroes do."

Barney cleared his throat and continued, "When I was about your age, my pa told me about a great baseball player named Joe Jackson. He played for the White Sox. 'Shoeless Joe' they called him, because he once played without shoes due to some ornery blisters. He got the suckers from breaking in a new pair of spikes. I still have a picture in my head of him in the outfield diving to make miraculous catches. But what my pa never told me, what I found out later, was that he was supposedly involved in a scandal. With gamblers. During the World Series of 1919. Folks said that Joe sold out, threw the win to Cincinnati."

Scandal. Gamblers. The words hung heavy in the air.

"So he was a bad guy?" Whitaker asked.

"Gee, Whitaker, *I* don't think so. It's one of those things that's hard to say. But maybe it shows that there aren't any real heroes." Barney's voice wasn't very persuasive.

"But what about super heroes?"

"Super heroes," Barney said, thinking deeply. "I suppose that they're a unique breed." He picked his teeth. "You mean like Frogman?"

"Yup. He is real, isn't he?"

As much as he felt that he ought to, Barney didn't have the heart to shatter Whitaker's illusion. "You believe in him—sometimes that's enough," Barney managed to say.

Whitaker's ears wanted to hear more. His eyes said so.

Unsure of what would happen or what his next move should be, but unwilling to admit defeat, Barney smiled and said, "Yes. Yes, Frogman is real. And I have a feeling that you'll get a sign real soon. Just be patient and keep your parents from worrying.

"Yes," Whitaker said, overcome with anticipation.

"I'd better get rolling," Barney said. He moved quickly down the block, his mind a whirlpool of thought.

Whitaker wondered how long he'd have to wait for the sign. A day? A week? A month? He was certain that Frogman would come through, though. And waiting for something that's bound to happen isn't always bad. Whitaker stayed in the front yard a few minutes longer. He looked around—to the tower, the sky, down the block—just in case the sign was early. Whitaker saw nothing special or unusual. Absolutely nothing.

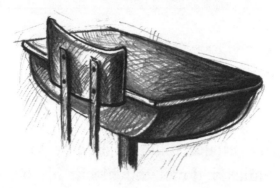

CHAPTER 12

Floor Poison

WHILE BARNEY WAS SUPPOSED TO BE casing up his mail, he was reading comic books. He was trying to brush up on his general knowledge of Frogman, with the hope of thinking of something to use as a sign for Whitaker. Barney had a sizable stack of *The Adventures of Frogman* comics on his desk. He shared them with the other carriers, all of them having a lighthearted, laughter-filled morning until Orson heard and put a damper on the happy ruckus. From then on, Barney did his research privately.

While Whitaker was supposed to be doing his multiplication tables, he was doodling pictures of Frogman and the water tower. Miss Smathers didn't value his artistic energy and as punishment made him stay in for the afternoon recess. Felicity stayed in too. She had the sniffles.

"That often happens when you try to adapt to a new part of the country and its climate," Felicity said with a cough. "My father told me so."

There was something about the way she talked—the words she used, her continuous smile—that left Whitaker uncertain.

"I'll just be gone a few minutes," Miss Smathers said. "Whitaker, I want your multiplication tables finished by the time I get back. And, Felicity, please wipe your nose."

Miss Smathers handed Felicity a tissue and

left Room 103 to gulp down a cup of coffee and as many cinnamon rolls as she could without appearing too gluttonous to the other faculty members.

After 3 × 9, Whitaker put down his pencil and looked at Felicity. "This is boring," he said bashfully.

"Not really," Felicity answered. She was tearing her used tissue into tiny pieces and putting them around the inside of Cynthia's desk.

"What are you doing that for?" Whitaker asked.

"Because Cynthia sits behind me and ties crayons in my hair. Now maybe she'll catch my germs and get a *really* bad cold, so she has to stay home. Forever."

Whitaker walked to the window. Jeff was stealing a ball from some little first graders. And Gordy was coming in first in the races across the length of the playground. Whitaker was the fastest in the class; he wished that he was out there, winning. "This *is* boring," he said.

"Not for long," Felicity announced, smiling.

When Felicity finished with her tissue, she stood on her desk and yelled, "Look out!"

"What's the matter?" Whitaker asked.

"Are you blind? The floor is poison. If you touch it, you'll die."

Whitaker jumped onto the nearest desk.

"Listen," Felicity explained, "the floor is quicksand and you have to get to the blackboard to rescue the sleeping princess."

"What princess?" Whitaker asked.

"The eraser, you know, the princess," Felicity answered. "But remember, you can't touch the floor."

Whitaker jumped from desk to desk until he got near the blackboard. He tried to reach the eraser, but he couldn't. "What am I supposed to do now?" he asked.

"That's your problem."

Whitaker opened the desk (it was Susan's)

and grabbed a reading workbook and a notebook. He tossed them in front of him onto the floor. He stepped on them until he could reach the eraser. "There," he said triumphantly, "the princess is rescued."

"Now it's my turn," Felicity said. "You have to give me directions."

"Okay," Whitaker said. "The floor is bear blood and Miss Smathers's desk is Frogman's spaceship. That's where you have to get if you want to be safe."

Following Whitaker's idea, Felicity jumped up to the front of the room, gathering reading workbooks on her way. When she got to the last desk, she lay the workbooks in front of her, one by one, all the way to the "spaceship."

"I did it!" Felicity shouted. She smiled. And sneezed.

Whitaker thought that her teeth were the biggest and straightest and whitest he'd ever seen in his life. She should make toothpaste commercials, he said to himself.

"Now," Whitaker said, "let's just chase each other. First one to touch the floor is the loser."

They both armed themselves with workbooks and notebooks and textbooks and folders, and jumped all around the classroom.

Whitaker was in the middle of a giant leap when the bell rang. He slipped on a folder as he landed. He touched the floor. "I guess I'm dead," he said.

"Who cares?" Felicity replied. "Everyone's coming in and we have a mess to clean up. Come on."

Felicity and Whitaker picked up all the workbooks and notebooks and textbooks and folders and tossed them into the closest desks. They didn't have enough time to put them in the right places.

"There," Whitaker said, "at least the room *looks* like it should." He sat down at his desk and started to work on his multiplication tables again.

Felicity sat down at her desk. She wiped

her nose with her finger, then folded her hands in front of her.

Miss Smathers entered the classroom. Icing covered her upper lip and chin. "Well, you two are certainly being quiet. That's what I like."

"I didn't *quite* finish," Whitaker said, eyes innocent.

"That's all right, Whitaker," Miss Smathers said as she brushed crumbs off her blouse. "I'm just so pleased to see you working hard for a change."

Whitaker turned around to look at Felicity. They smirked.

Jeff and Gordy and the other students started filing into the classroom, still excited from recess.

"Settle down, children," Miss Smathers said, loud and clear. "Now everyone open your desks and take out your reading workbooks. We have a *lot* of work to do this afternoon."

Did they ever!

CHAPTER 13

Passing Time

FLOOR POISON BECAME a good way to pass the time while waiting for the sign from Frogman. Whitaker taught Jeff and Gordy how to play. And that's what they did most nights after school. They played it at Jeff's house until they broke his mother's antique Wedgwood vase. They played it at Gordy's house until they knocked over Mr. Lucas's stuffed and mounted deer, chipping its antler. And they played it at Whitaker's house until the time they jumped so hard that they ruined Mrs. Murphy's famous soufflé, which she was preparing for her bridge club. Usually her masterpiece was as tall as a top hat; that day it was as flat as the cow-pies that Whitaker and his cousins used as bases when they played ball at the annual family reunion at Uncle Harold's farm.

All of these incidents were accidents, of course. Nonetheless, Floor Poison had to be eliminated from Whitaker's things-to-do-while-waiting-for-Frogman repertoire. Among others, this included what Whitaker called "Zebra-zooming." This had started one night, years earlier, as an amusement when Mr. Murphy ran into the hardware store to pick up some nails that he needed. Mrs. Murphy stayed in the car with baby Whitaker on her lap. Whitaker reached for the steering wheel and made noises that a car might make. Mr. Murphy let him do the same when Mrs. Murphy went into the grocery store. And the game caught on.

Even now Whitaker would sit in the Zebra and imagine that he was driving. Turning the wheel. Pushing the directional lever up and down. Saying, "Zooooom! Zooooom!" Whitaker couldn't reach the brake or gas pedal yet, but it didn't matter. In his own way, he was going very fast. Rounding hairpin turns. Jumping caverns. Running red lights. The whole bit. All the while, he was on the lookout for Frogman. But never a trace did he see.

During this period Whitaker sorted his baseball cards and reorganized his bug collection alphabetically (that is, *A*nt, *B*eetle, *C*rushed ant, *D*ragonfly, *E*lmer Ant, *G*lued-together ant, and so on). He also went to Horlick's Field.

Whitaker ambled through the field, swishing the now tall, brownish grass, searching for Frogman's footprints around the water tower and near the creek. In the sand on the creek's bank, he saw dog pawprints and cat pawprints and tennis-shoe footprints and what he thought were beaver pawprints. But none resembled those of his hero.

Walking west, Whitaker discovered some new graffiti scribbled on the sideboards of Horlick's Bridge. He studied the words. They appeared freshly painted. The messy letters spelled things like "Babe Ruth for President," "Go Brewers!," and "Shoeless Joe Lives," in dark blue paint. But there were no messages from Frogman.

Whitaker found a rusty key and a 1948 penny and a feather and his lost batting glove. And he found Barney.

"Well, Whitaker, fancy meeting you here," Barney said, getting to his feet. He had been crouching by the edge of the creek.

"What are you doing, Barney?"

"I stopped on my way home from work to look for rocks. My granddaughter in Florida collects them. And I promised her that I'd send her a few from Wisconsin. No collection would be complete without them. Don't you think?"

Barney held out his hand to show Whitaker his findings. Whitaker didn't think that the stones were anything special until Barney pointed out their subtle coloring and fine shapes.

"If you look close enough, there's a world of things to see in something like a stone." Barney reached into his uniform shirt pocket that by now was dirty and damp and spotted with dark blue paint, the same shade as that on the bridge. He retrieved a small green object. "I also discovered this piece of glass that the creek has worked on. Rounded its edges. Softened it. It's no diamond, but its beauty comes darn close in my estimation."

Perhaps it was the mood he was in, but the piece of glass didn't interest Whitaker. But he did wonder about the dark blue spatters on Barney's shirt and the can of paint on the ground near his uniform jacket. Whitaker tried to picture Barney writing on the bridge. He couldn't. He thought that only junior high kids got to do that.

"Anyway, Whitaker, what are *you* doing in what's left of this town's wilderness?" Barney asked.

"I came looking for Frogman. Or at least a sign from him."

Barney could have guessed that. But he hadn't decided yet what he could do to get out of the predicament that he had gotten himself into. "I'd ask how progress was going," Barney said, "but I have a feeling that it would be a wasted question."

Barney was tempted to ask Whitaker exactly what kind of sign would satisfy his curiosity, but he didn't. He wanted to solve this on his own. After all, what's a challenge for?

The clouds that had been rolling in since early afternoon started to drop rain. A fine mist soon turned into a cold, steady pelting.

Whitaker and Barney said good-bye to each other, then speedily headed in their respective directions home. Whitaker momentarily forgot about Frogman—he didn't miss a single puddle or clogged sewer from the field to his front porch. Neither did Barney.

CHAPTER 14

A Change of Plans

THE FOLLOWING SATURDAY Barney had a hard time concentrating on his work. All his energy was being spent thinking of what he could tell Whitaker. Because it was Saturday and there was no school, Barney figured that today would be the day to break the bad news to his buddy. After an agonizing week —and no ideas to use as a sign from Frogman—Barney concluded that the best thing to do was to explain everything about the letters. That they weren't real. And neither was Frogman.

As he approached the Murphy house, Barney's heart grew heavy, beating fast and hard. He reached into his sack for their mail. There was another postcard, a gigantic one, from Aunt Nancy and Uncle Iggie. That was all. Barney read the postcard with the intention of momentarily forgetting his dilemma.

It said:

Dear ones,

This is what Central Park looks like from an airplane. Reminds me of a fuzzy green Band-aid in the middle of giant boxes. Anyway, we walked through here. You wouldn't believe all the people! Some running, some walking, some fighting, some sleeping.

We saw some roller-skaters, and Uncle Iggie had the notion to try it. Well, he did just fine until he decided to hot-dog it. He was going backward on one foot—and what do you suppose happens? He knocked himself into one of those mime characters. Ended up with two broken legs. The mime was okay— at least he didn't say anything. So now we just sit in the hotel room and eat and look out the window. (We've made friends with a pigeon family.) But maybe this is all a blessing in disguise, because I've already crocheted 14 telephone book covers to use as Christmas gifts.

Love always,
Nancy and Iggie

Funny as it was, Barney didn't even smile. "Look what I've got," Whitaker called, when he saw Barney. It was the Frogman Utility Pen that Whitaker had sent for with box tops from Colonel Cornflakes. "It's not the sign, but it's neat. I got it this morning. A man in a big brown delivery truck brought it."

"My, my," Barney said, examining it.

"It squirts water. It tells time. And best of all, it writes in gold ink that glows in the dark," Whitaker recited, as if he were a salesman. "And remember," Whitaker added, thinking of the advertising on the cereal box, "something written in gold lasts forever."

Just then Mr. Murphy came out onto the porch with a jacket for Whitaker. "Put this on, Whit. It's chilly out here." Looking at Barney, he said, in greeting, "Morning, Barney."

"Morning," Barney answered, trying to smile. He handed Mr. Murphy the postcard. "That's some pen Whitaker has there."

Mr. Murphy shook his head and frowned. "I'll say," he said sarcastically. "Barney, you wouldn't believe all the trouble a little pen like that can cause."

Whitaker didn't want to hang around—he didn't like the direction in which the conversation was leaning. "Bye, Barney," he said, as he ran into the backyard to practice pitching.

Barney waved.

"Oh, Barney," Mr. Murphy said, obviously flustered. "Some days, I tell you, I don't know." He nervously tapped the postcard against his leg. "Because of that little pen, Whitaker has gotten the crazy idea that Frogman is going to write *him* a message in gold. As big as a house, he says. In 'extra-ultra-fluorescent letters,' he says. To prove that Frogman is real. And something written in gold, he says, lasts forever.

"Barney, Frogman is a *cartoon character*," Mr. Murphy continued, "and my Whitaker has to go and believe in him. Why?"

Barney grinned. "That's the way it goes with kids," he said, his face starting to glow.

"And that's what tomorrows are for. By then, things are generally forgotten or resolved. Sometimes *unbelievably* so."

"*Tomorrow?* This kind of thing has been going on for *weeks*." Mr. Murphy scratched his head. "All I can say is I envy you today, Barney—all your kids are grown-up." His eyes scanning the water tower, Mr. Murphy added, "I could tell you stories you'd *never* believe."

"I bet I would," Barney whispered. In a matter of seconds, he was already two houses away. He hurried through the rest of his route, faster than he ever had.

That night on the way home from work, Barney stopped at the hardware store to buy five cans of gold, glow-in-the-dark paint. The best plan of his life was beginning to form in his mind. And there was no time to lose.

CHAPTER 15

The Day Before Tomorrow

BECAUSE BARNEY HAD to attend to his plan, he couldn't watch the televised Brewer game that night. It was the first game that he had missed all season. But it would prove worth it, in a way he hadn't counted on.

Mr. Murphy and Whitaker watched, though. As usual, Mr. Murphy had beer. Whitaker had grape Kool-Aid. And they both had potato chips.

"I hope we win," Whitaker said, cramming a whole potato chip into his mouth.

"I do too," Mr. Murphy agreed.

Whitaker was keeping score on the back of his reading workbook with his Frogman Utility Pen. The gold ink was as shiny as ever. In between batters, Whitaker worked on a drawing of Frogman in a baseball cap, with the water tower in the background.

Mr. Murphy glanced over every few minutes to look at the drawing. But he didn't say a word.

During a commercial for EXPENSE credit cards, Whitaker asked, "Dad, how do they get the ripples in the potato chips?"

"I suppose a machine does it," Mr. Murphy answered. "But I never really thought about it before."

Whitaker decided to try to separate the ripples. It didn't work. All that he managed to make was a pile of potato chip crumbs. But he kept trying.

After a two-run homer by Cecil Cooper, Mr. Murphy turned to Whitaker, clapping. "All right!" he cheered. That's when Mr. Murphy spotted the potato chip crumbs all over the carpet. "Whitaker, your mother will not love that. Why don't you get a napkin and clean it up?"

When Whitaker got up from the floor, he knocked over his glass of Kool-Aid.

"Oh, Whitaker," Mr. Murphy said. "When you get that napkin, how about bringing back a wet dishrag too, to wipe up this grape mess someone made here?"

"Frogman could just zap it away," Whitaker said, leaving the den.

"Well, you're not Frogman—he doesn't exist," Mr. Murphy shouted after Whitaker. "And hurry up!"

While Whitaker was in the kitchen, Mr.

Murphy reached for the Frogman Utility Pen to see what time it was. He couldn't get it to work, so he shook it and tapped it against the end table. Something snapped. The spring shot across the room. The cartridge cracked. The pen squirted water. And then it leaked gold ink all over the sofa.

"Oh, no," Mr. Murphy said. He closed his eyes, threw back his head, and grunted something like "Urrgh!"

"What a mess, Daddy," Molly observed, matter-of-factly, as she pushed her doll carriage into the den to see what was on TV. "Wait till Mommy sees it."

"Hurry up, Whitaker!" Mr. Murphy yelled, trying to ignore Molly. "What are you doing, *making* the dishrag?"

Whitaker dashed into the den with the dishrag and a napkin. "Frogman to the rescue!" he shouted. He had cleaned up his mess before he saw the broken pen.

"What happened?" Whitaker asked, staring at a pool of gold ink. "You wrecked it!"

"I had an accident too. Just as you did," Mr. Murphy said. "I'm really sorry, son," he added softly.

"But, Da-a-ad, it'll take *eight* more boxtops to get another one. *Eight!*"

"Listen, Whitaker," Mr. Murphy said, ready to give up, "I'll help you eat the lousy cereal if it's that important. But after all, it's just a pen."

"*Just a pen?*"

"Just a pen."

Silence. Except for Whitaker mumbling, "Eight, eight, eight . . ."

After counting to ten, Mr. Murphy motioned with his head and patted the sofa cushion, inviting Whitaker to sit down. "I think we should try to forget this whole thing. So come on, Whit, let's watch the rest of the game. All right?"

Whitaker grabbed the broken pen and stormed up to his room without saying a word. He didn't care anymore who would win the game. Placing the pen, now in six pieces, on his bookshelf, he wondered only if he'd *ever* get his sign from Frogman.

"What's all the fuss?" Mrs. Murphy called to her husband. "I could hear you all the way in the laundry room."

"Just a bit of baseball excitement, I guess," Mr. Murphy answered.

"Well, good, who's winning?" Mrs. Murphy asked.

Mr. Murphy sighed. "Definitely not me."

As he tried to clean the gold ink stain from the sofa, Mr. Murphy remembered what Whitaker had said about gold—how it lasts forever. He hoped that it really didn't, at least on sofas. Mr. Murphy also remembered what Barney had said earlier that day about tomorrows, how things are generally forgotten then. Only problem, Mr. Murphy thought, is that tomorrow never really comes.

CHAPTER 16

On and On

WELL, MARVELOUSLY ENOUGH, tomorrow *did* come. And it was Sunday.

Sunday mornings weren't as good as Saturday mornings in Whitaker's opinion. But they were better than Monday, Tuesday, Wednesday, Thursday, or Friday mornings. Sunday morning meant a big breakfast with the whole family and something extra, like crullers or pecan kringle or doughnuts. It meant no school. It meant a chance to explore at Horlick's Field, or to get a game of baseball going if the weather cooperated. It meant a whole day to eat Colonel Cornflakes, which meant a new box of cereal and another box top toward a new Utility Pen. It meant time to wait for Frogman. And it also meant the Sunday funnies, where Frogman always appeared in full color on the front page.

Like an alarm clock, the newspaper hitting the front porch woke up Whitaker without fail. Then he, in turn, woke up Molly, who woke up Mr. and Mrs. Murphy.

A sleepy parade, they shuffled down the steps. Molly and Mr. and Mrs. Murphy stayed in the kitchen to start breakfast. Whitaker went out to get the paper so he could read the comics first.

Whitaker opened the front door, and before he even located the paper, he stood paralyzed, facing the water tower. His eyes grew large. He blinked them once. He blinked them twice. But the enormous message didn't vanish. It was as real as the water tower itself. The big F was outlined in gold, and following it were more letters. They spelled "FROGMAN LIVES . . ."

As big as a house.

Written in gold.

To last forever.

"Mom! Dad! Molly!" Whitaker cried as he ran into the kitchen. "Come here! Now!"

The family, reacting to Whitaker's excitement, hastily went out to the porch after him.

Whitaker pointed to the tower.

"Oh, my word," Mrs. Murphy said, squinting.

"Oh brother," Mr. Murphy said, shaking his head.

"What does it say?" Molly asked, jumping up and down.

"It says 'FROGMAN LIVES . . .'" Whitaker replied proudly.

"What are the three dots for?" Molly asked.

"That means on and on," Mrs. Murphy answered.

"On and on," Molly repeated. "And on and on and on."

The four of them just stayed there a while, wondering.

After a minute or two, Whitaker noticed that the gold letters weren't straight and even like the F. They didn't look much different from the graffiti scrawled on the side of Horlick's Bridge. In fact, this message and the ones on the bridge seemed more alike the longer he looked.

Shoot, Whitaker thought, everything making sense all at once. Everything. There was no wondering now. He kicked the porch railing, feeling that he had been tricked. Not liking it. Crazy old mailman.

Then he remembered Molly. And how he always played along with the idea of Santa

Claus and the Easter Bunny. "Helping her grow up," his parents called it. And maybe, Whitaker thought, this is the same kind of thing. Only with Barney doing the "helping." Not me. Crazy old Barney.

Suddenly a smile broke across Whitaker's face. I know, he thought, I won't even let on to Barney. Just let him think I believe. Good old Barney.

"You're going to write to Frogman again, aren't you?" Molly asked anxiously, now totally convinced of Frogman's existence and his presence in Franklinville. "Aren't you?"

A long silence passed before Whitaker answered.

"I doubt it," he finally said, smiling. "I don't have to anymore."